For Dana on her second Halloween   —*E. B.*
For my mother   —*J. B.*

Clarion Books
a Houghton Mifflin Company imprint
215 Park Avenue South, New York, NY 10003
Text copyright © 1986 by Eve Bunting
Illustrations copyright © 1986 by Jan Brett Studio, Inc.
For information about permission to reproduce
selections from this book, write to Permissions,
Houghton Mifflin Company, 2 Park Street, Boston, MA 02108
Printed in the USA
HOR 10 9 8
Library of Congress Cataloging-in-Publication Data
Bunting, Eve, 1928-
Scary, scary Halloween.
Summary: A band of trick-or-treaters and a mother
cat and her kittens spend a very scary Halloween.
[1. Halloween—Fiction.   2. Cats—Fiction.
3. Stories in rhyme]   I. Brett, Jan, ill.   II. Title.
PZ8.3.B92Sc   1986   (E)   86-2642
ISBN 0-89919-414-1   PA ISBN 0-89919-799-X

Eve Bunting

Scary, Scary Halloween

pictures by Jan Brett

Clarion Books
New York

I peer outside, there's something there
That makes me shiver, spikes my hair.
It must be Halloween.

A skeleton, with bones so white
They gleam and glimmer in the night,
Has come for Halloween.

A ghost goes trailing, drifting by
With sunken mouth and sunken eye.
Ghosts rise on Halloween.

"Little ones, stay safe inside!
It's best to stay at home and hide
On hallowed Halloween."

A vampire and a werewolf prowl.
One growls a growl, one howls a howl
In praise of Halloween.

Two witches, grinning witchy grins,
Have pointy hats and pointy chins.
They're here for Halloween.

"Cover eye and cover ear,
Nightmares walk the streets of fear
On dreaded Halloween."

Goblins, gremlins skip and leap,
They never rest, they never sleep,
They're glad it's Halloween.

A devil prances, fiery red,
With horns asprouting from his head.
He knows it's Halloween.

Thunder, thunder up above!
"What is it, mother?" "Shh, my love!
It's just the thump of creature feet,
A creature in a winding sheet.
His claws are dragging on the floor,
He's crashing, smashing at the door!"

"Will he find us here, below?"
"Shh, my love, I cannot know."

"Trick or Treat? It's Halloween!
Am I the scariest thing you've seen?
Tonight? On Halloween?"

"He didn't see us, didn't care.
We weren't the ones he'd come to scare
This night of Halloween."

It's quiet now, the monster's gone,
The streets are ours until the dawn.
We're out, we prowlers of the night
Who snap and snarl and claw and bite.

We stalk the shadows, dark, unseen...
Goodbye 'til next year, Halloween.